SKY CAPTAIN ADVENTURES 3
John Pirillo

BLASTED THROUGH TIME

Trans-Timeline Effect

F lashes of light smashed into his helmet, blinding him, as he continued to accelerate. His helmet readouts were all over the place, badgering him to slow down, with multiple warning lights firing up, threatening to shut down his power.

He ignored the warnings.

Hadn't done any good to acknowledge them in the past, why waste his strength on it now.

The suit seemed to have a will of its own once the Trans-Timeline effect kicked in.

He just didn't care anymore. He wanted to go home. He'd had enough of this time stream business. Being hurled about from one time period to another like a helpless puppet on a string, pulled by some kind of cruel invisible puppeteer.

He didn't want to think God. He couldn't go that far. But he had to wonder why at times this was happening. And so far he just couldn't come up with anything beyond; his suit had one purpose and him another.

He kicked with his feet, as if that might propel him faster. Make the Trans-Timeline stretch faster and snap him to wherever it had in mind so he could get on with his life again.

Hopefully back to World War Two in his own timeline, but if not that, at least not dumping him in some deserted hellhole where humanity had blasted itself out of existence and only zombies remained.

Yeah, he'd been there done that.

He checked his speed again.

Not registering.

If readouts could break, this one would have exploded. According to Einstein the only possible way he could break through timelines was if he traveled at the speed of light.

Theory or Reality, Take your Pick

Morgan sat down opposite Einstein at the cafeteria table he was puttering away at. The man was modeling something that made no sense to Morgan at the moment.

Einstein held it up for him to look at more closely. "Impossible, yes?"

Morgan checked it out closely. The strip of thick paper, doubled over and elongated with tape sticking it together, didn't seem to have a beginning or an end to it.

"How in the world did you do that, Doc?"

Barry shuffled up with two cups of coffee, set one down for Morgan and one for him.

"Magic," Barry said, then ambled off again.

"Think cocoa, Barry."

"I'd definitely like to thank her," Barry quipped over his shoulder.

Al...short for Albert...grinned. "Your partner never lets up, does he?"

"It's war trauma. He can't deal with the anguish associated with killing any other way. At least he treats his women with respect and dumps them gracefully."

Al laughed. "I'm sure they appreciate that."

Morgan grinned. "Actually. Not. Two of them tried to blow him up. Lucky for Bear, I caught them planting the grenades in the head."

Al gave him a surprised look. "You both could have been killed."

"Didn't happen though, did it?"

Al nodded. He set his twisted shape down.

"Well."

"Well what?"

"Question. The question you have to ask me."

Morgan studied the older man thoughtfully a moment, then nodded. "Okay. Way I see it, time travel is pretty shaky as a science."

"Got that."

"And I never know when or where I'll end up because of that."

"Got that too."

Al waited for the real question patiently and Morgan satisfied him.

"Then how in the hell am I ever to get control of this damn thing I go through. Lives depend on me."

Al put a hand on Morgan's arm to calm him down.

Morgan sighed.

"Sorry, didn't mean to explode."

"Son, you've had that one coming a long time."

"Well?"

"Well what?"

"Doc, why not?"

Al scooted the complex strip of paper towards Morgan.

"Look closely at it, and then you tell me."

Morgan lifted the paperwork up and examined it more closely.

Barry returned with a cup of cocoa and three plates of eggs, sausage and toast for the three of them in the crook of his other arm.

"I love you," Al told him.

Barry grinned.

"Sorry, Doc, you're just not my type."

Al laughed.

Morgan eyed Barry a moment. "What do you see here, Bear?"

"A helluva lot of confusion and not much sense, but overall a lot of paper folded over and hooked together nice and neat. Good job, Doc."

"Thanks."

Al lifted is cocoa, took a sip, made a face. "Not sweet enough."

He grabbed the sugar bowl on the table and dumped half into the cocoa.

Barry and Morgan let out whistles.

Al eyed them sternly. "You're not the only ones who have anguish, you know."

They all broke into laughter.

Barry eyed the paper contraption again. "Right off hand, Cap, I'd say this was symbolic of time."

Al gave Barry a surprised look, as did Morgan.

Barry shrugged and tore into his breakfast. Between mouthfuls he mumbled, "Consider the creator and your question, Cap."

"Gotcha!" Cap agreed with a nod.

"So what does this have to do with time travel, Doc?"

He shoved the paper creation back to Al, who set it to his right, then began eating as well. Between bites he said, "I know it's not as simple as you'd like, but it explains basically what you're going through."

"Which is?" Morgan asked, as he took a hit of coffee, and then swished it in his mouth, savoring its taste.

"That time is too complex to understand on a linear basis."

"And?"

Barry looked up from his eggs he had been battering with his butter knife, adding jam to them and waited for Al's reply.

"The only way we'll ever understand what you're experiencing, Captain, is when you discover the answer. It hurts my brain trying to figure it out."

Barry laughed so hard and loud that he spit out his food all over the place.

Time Construct

Doc tried to make it as easy on Morgan as he could, explaining that somehow he would always end up back where he started from, because all the pieces of paper in his construct were interconnected.

"Energy cannot be created or destroyed," Al explained.

"And?"

"Your suit and you...somehow are connected."

He shoved the paper construction towards Morgan again. "Just like these strips of paper are all connected. They appear to be in different spots, but..."

Al picked up the construction and gently inverted it, so that now all the strips were facing new angles and sides.

Barry set down three strips of bacon he was about to shovel into his mouth. "That's a nifty trick, Doc, where'd you learn it?"

"China."

"I hear they got beautiful women there."

"I wouldn't know; I was married at the time. Still am. And happily," he told Barry, with the hint of a scolding in his voice.

Barry ignored it. "Jazzes me anyway, Doc. I'd love to meet a Geisha girl someday."

"They're not called Geisha girls in China, Bear?" Morgan explained.

"Long as they have olive skin and oval eyes, I'm on for it," Barry said, ignoring Al and Morgan.

Morgan eyed Al again. "So when does this all come to an end?"

Al looked suddenly quite ominously quiet and somber.

"Doc! Level with me!" Morgan demanded, feeling his anger arousing again.

Barry solved the building crisis by dumping his extra sausage onto Morgan's plate. "I'm going back for more bacon. It's really good today."

Al gave him a look of thanks.

Barry winked and departed with his empty plate.

"When?" Morgan demanded. His anger gone, replaced by an empty feeling in his heart.

Al shrugged. "Your guess is as good as mine."

"Give me something!" Morgan begged.

"Okay," Barry agreed, dumping more sausage on Morgan's plate. "Eat up, Cap. Mission control just sent for us. We got five, and then we're on for it."

Al yet again looked relieved as Barry winked at him when Morgan wasn't looking.

Morgan eyed the huge heap of sausage on his plate and then gave up. He began forking them into his mouth, two at a time.

Trans-Timeline Effect

The one thing that always amazed Morgan, was how clear his memories became when he trans-lined. It was like he was reliving them all over again...in reality.

Somehow, they always triggered an awakening of some kind in Morgan, sort of like when Sherlock Holmes would go "Ah-ha!" and then go straight for the villain and solve the crime.

The mystical lights that spattered beyond outstretched arms and hands continued to blast at him, veering off before they touched him. Balls of explosive light would shatter into non-existence ahead of him. Bubbles of time would pass by.

He could see different points in his own lifetime briefly as they passed.

When he was a baby and took his first few steps.

His mother changing his diapers.

His dad going off to war in World War One.

His first high school sweetheart.

His pet frog, Dewey Dimples.

The football he kicked over the goalpost, winning the game for his team.

Morgan didn't bother to look at his speed. Didn't have to. He was accelerating. He couldn't feel any subsequent pressuring on his body. None of his equipment was failing; though he feared someday it might.

Everything was perfect, except he didn't know for sure when or where he would pop out next. Would he return to his own timeline, or to the most recent one he and Al had discussed the time construct.

Still, all in all, he knew it didn't matter. When the Trans-Timeline effect kicked in it was usually at unpredictable moments, when his suit was failing, explosive situations. When his emotions were tight as too tight a rubber band, or...

"Damn!" He cursed.

He slung his right hand out, as if to smash his own stupidity. A light came on in his brain.

All this time it had been staring him in the face; in Doc's face.

Emotions!

Emotions were energy. And energy can neither be created nor destroyed. Hence, his Trans-Timeline timeline transitions were being directed by his emotions.

Then he could have kicked himself further. "How in the hell am I supposed to do that?" He asked the timelines smashing past him.

"How?"

He had been blasted back and forth through time, from World War Two to World War Three where the Nazi Empire ruled supreme. He had lost the only woman he loved and found a new love in the future. He had been shot down and wounded, frozen and revived, then armed with a powerful suit of armor that ancient medieval knights would have considered to have godlike powers. But none of that mattered. Wars seemed to be the norm in all the trans-time lines he had traveled to and through. Maybe there were places where mankind had learned to get along, but he hadn't found one, or at least been thrown into one.

Yet.

For a brief moment his more stoic nature began to crumble. "I don't want to be Superman," he sighed.

Exiled from his dying world and trying to make up for his loss by nurturing another civilization. He wasn't the Superman type. He was just an air force pilot who got drafted to fly an armored suit that flew faster than sound."

Yeah. And how did that work for you? He asked himself.

So? Science was great. He had great pals in Einstein, Edison and Tesla, but he would have given his right leg or arm to be back in the world of war he had left behind. His original timeline. Where his lost love was probably still waiting for him and he would never arrive.

Or maybe not.

He believed in God.

If this craziness was all part of God's Plan, wouldn't it make sense that when Morgan was blasting between times, that God would give his old pals and sweetheart a placebo to heal the rift in time and maybe even in their hearts?

You bet He would, Morgan thought, the idea taking a firm grip on his brain. It only made sense.

He snorted.

Something has to make sense, Damnit!

Then he plugged in the missing part of the equation for fixing his absence in the various times.

Me!

Lately, he had begun to wonder if the Trans-Timeline was shipping other versions of himself to the time streams he left to take up his position in that timeline and do what he might have done as that timeline unfolded.

When he talked with Barry about it on the first timeline, Barry didn't think so, because no one had shown up when he had trans-lined into the alternate Nazi future, where Hitler ruled as a disembodied brain. So if not that one, maybe others? Maybe there was no rhyme or reason to him and his friendships, but maybe there was a greater force. God or whatever...some kind of guiding intelligence that was using him as a knight on its gigantic board of chess to equalize the worlds in turmoil.

He smiled.

Maybe someday someone would make a movie about a man lost in time.

Maybe.

If so, he wished they would mind their own business and leave him out of it. He knew once the war or wars were over. When his part was done, he'd just want to have a nice acre near a small stream and just dangle his bare feet in the waters and suck lemonade for the rest of his life.

No more complications.

Maybe even a dog or two. A cat.

A wife?

His heart hurt at that thought. Would that ever happen? Would he live to see it?

He came out of his musings and examined his readouts again. Same. Crazy!

He shut his eyes.

He was so tired.

God only knew how long this transition would take. If he could just catch a few moments of sleep. The suit would alert him if anything was off.

He shut his eyes.

"Cap!" Bear's voice screamed in his ear.

A burst of light outside illuminated the inside of his helmet and even through his closed eyelids he could see lights and colors beyond imagination.

He opened his eyes when the lights dimmed again. He was heading straight for the moon. And that it was growing larger and larger. Then he dared to look at his speed. He closed his eyes, blinked twice, and then looked again. Impossible! He was not just going faster than the speed of sound; he was traveling faster than any missile ever constructed. Even in future timelines!

He was certain he had already broken free of the Earth's gravitational pull, once he began spotting isolated chunks of rock...meteorites...in low orbit that weren't falling into the atmosphere.

Einstein had called it the perfect balance between gravity and the sun. The earth's pull and the Sun's gravitational pull. He hadn't invented a name for it, so Cap called it the Belt of Hercules, the spot where Earth's gravity no longer pulled anything down, but also, nothing was pulled away either.

He was tempted to see if the theory held and he would just float there in the Belt, but his determination to free himself of the barbaric future that lay on the Earth below was too powerful. Yes, he could have stayed like the older Sky Captain he had left behind. And maybe the two of them could have made a difference.

Maybe the American Sky Captain he spared would remember that not all Americans were cannibals and ruthless murderers like the world he was leaving behind was full of. Maybe a tiny spark of rebellion would be planted in his soul, and America could possibly change over the years. He didn't know. He didn't have the patience to find out. If he was stuck there as the other Sky Captain, maybe yes then.

The other had made his choice. He acted determined. But Morgan could tell the man had a great deal of remorse for his choice, probably remembered the woman and friends he had lost because of the choice, even as Morgan now felt.

"Okay, Baby!" Morgan sweet talked his Sky Captain suit. "Let's see what you're really made of!" Morgan gave the suit every ounce of power it had and it had a lot. Usually, he kept it restrained at about five percent power levels. Now he raised it to the maximum.

The tremendous force of the acceleration caused him to black out at the same time as every warning sensor and sound in his suit went berserk!

Warnings Ignored

"Under no conditions, Morgan." Al told him, seated in his classic pose of pipe in one hand and leg crossed over the other, his fuzzy hair flying in orbit above his eyebrows. "Under none whatsoever are you to ever unleash the full force of your power unit."

Morgan grinned at Al, egging him on, teasing the old man...who at thirty something was getting ancient in Morgan's eyes. "Afraid of me coming back as a milkshake?"

Al didn't bite. "No. Afraid of you becoming one with the universe!" He made a gesture of boom with his hands, and then waited for Morgan to respond.

Morgan had gotten a cold chill when Al demonstrated what happened.

"Hey tap toes!" Barry greeted Morgan with his favorite tease, dropping at the table next to Al and Morgan, hugging a mug of coffee between his strong hands. "What's up, brothers?"

Al's eyes twinkled. "We were just discussing my new theory...E=MCSquared."

"Oh, isn't that the one where everything turns to atoms?"

"Oh, much smaller than that." Al explained with an amused look on his face. He got up and sauntered off, not looking back or saying goodbye.

"Smart man, but lacking in social graces," Barry noted, following the man with his eyes. He looked back at Morgan. "Takes all kinds, I guess."

"Not that bad, Bear. The old man's just got a lot of Barry's in the fuel at the same time."

"Boom!" Barry laughed.

"Yeah. Pretty much, pal." Morgan rebutted. "But we should be so lucky to have that many burners in the mix, let alone one half as good."

Barry gave Morgan a narrow eyed look of suspicion. "You sniffing his tobacco when no one's looking?"

Morgan gave Barry a blank look.

Barry's eyes widened. "You didn't know?"

"Know what?"

"The old man..." He made gestures of someone smoking pot.

Morgan laughed. "You're nuts, Barry. He hates those kinds of things. He won't even touch beer, let alone anything stronger."

"Yeah. Now you know why I think he gets jazzed, Morgan. How else he going to turn off that crazy brain of his. Whoa-whoa. Train crash in the making if he doesn't."

Morgan laughed. "You're impossible!"

Barry smiled. "And you love every minute of it. Without me, you wouldn't know who to pick on or insult. And who would let you go out with their girlfriends but me?"

"Oh yeah. Like that's really a gesture of kindness. I have to patch them back together again after you break their hearts."

Barry winked. "Must be fun trying though."

Morgan shook his head. Stars swam in his vision. Billions of them!

"Morgan you're getting that far away look again," Barry blurted out, worried for his friend.

"Stars. Millions and millions of them." Morgan answered, trying to wave his hands through them to see if they would move or alter in some way. "They're all around me. Even in your face, Bear."

"Morgan, you're really starting to worry me!"

"Barry, can't you see them?" Morgan pleaded. "Even you are made of stars!"

Morgan looked at Barry again, trying to shake off any hallucination he might be having; but it wasn't. Bear was definitely this human shaped galaxy of stars that was giving him a frightened look.

"AL!" Barry screamed. "AL!"

Morgan grabbed his head, and then he saw that his arms were stars too.

Frightened, he let go and looked up at the sound of running feet. Before he saw two shapes similar to Al and Tesla running through a blazing tunnel of furious, burning orbs towards him.

"Morgan!" Bear shouted. "Hang on, pal!"

Morgan shut his eyes.

This was finally the end.

"You're too late, guys. But nice try."

Trans-Timelining Again

Morgan felt as if his body had turned into a burning stream of light. It shot forth into the cosmos, consuming everything in its path. Nothing was safe.

The moon hurtled at him, and then exploded into atoms.

He soared past Mars.

It exploded into millions of sparkling pieces.

"Come back to me!" Nurse Betty told him.

Base

"It's all right, Baby. It's all right." Nurse Betty told him, holding his head in her lap, where he lay on the concrete floor of the secret bunker. His Sky Captain suit was discarded to the right, smoking as if it had caught on fire.

Morgan knew better. He had flown through stars. And stars and stars. But not inside his suit!

"You're home, Baby!" She cried, her eyes filled with tears.

He reached a hand up, not believing what had just happened. He had time-lined without his suit. And yet, here he was, lying on the floor and his suit was next to him. Smoking for sure, but there all the same.

He finally looked into Betty's eyes. They were bloodshot and tear filled. "Hi Doll! You are sure a sight for sore eyes. And believe me, my eyes are plenty sore."

He could barely hold her in focus at first, but as his eyes watered, his vision began to clear. The stars which he had seen trying to overwhelm t his timeline and take him away were fading.

"Boop to you." She joked, and then burst into more tears.

He tried to sit up, and then groaned from the effort.

"It's all right, Baby. You don't have to move. You don't have to fly anymore. Just stay with me. Everything will be all right." She promised, kissing his cheeks with tear moist lips. "I promise you'll never have to go out there and fight again. Ever and ever and ever."

"And ever?" He asked with a grin, which somehow felt incredibly painful.

"And ever!" She said with finality.

Barry came running to where Morgan lay and scooted close. "Morgan, you old bag of bones. Where the hell have you been all these years?"

Morgan smiled weakly. It hurt. It hurt. It hurt. "Everywhere. Nowhere. In the stars! Out of the stars. Back in time. Forward in time. Fighting monsters. Nazis, you know the usual Superman stuff," he joked.

Then he felt his emotions began to well up. He couldn't hold back the pain he had been feeling with cheap jokes anymore. He began to sob.

Betty pulled him against her.

Barry dropped to the floor and put his arms around the both of them. "It's good to have you back, pal. Even if you look like shit!"

Morgan laughed. "Says the bag of."

Barry patted Morgan's head gently. "Now there's the man I know and Betty loves." He kissed the top of Morgan's head and then pulled away.

Morgan let out a groan.

Betty pulled him closer. "Where's it hurt, baby?"

"My chest."

"Get a doctor!" Shouted Barry.

The sound of running feet.

Barry touched Morgan gently across his chest, pressing his palms over that of Nurse Betty's. It felt good, but the pain didn't lessen. It increased.

Morgan screamed in pain and began to spasm.

"Hold him down, hold him down!" Betty ordered Barry.

Barry flattened Morgan and pinned him to the floor with his powerful arms. Morgan subsided.

A look of extreme acceptance came over his face.

Barry got off.

"Pal, what's wrong, talk to the Bear, will ya?"

"I guess I didn't make it after all, did I?"

He could hear the sound of Betty hollering and running feet, but it was fading as he looked into the face of the man he loved almost as much as Betty, but in a different way.

"What are you talking about, you fool!" Barry screamed, and then lowered his voice. "I'm sorry, Morgan, you just got me a bit wound up is all. Everything's fine. Fine!"

Betty dropped next to him.

Medics ripped his shirt off. They began checking his pulse and blood pressure.

Morgan didn't even feel them doing it. He looked at Betty and her eyes answered his questions about what was going on. His heart was quitting. "I didn't make it."

She shook her head. "No, you made it, baby. All the way back home. All the way!"

Morgan closed his eyes. "I think I can rest now."

"Morgan!" Betty shrieked.

"It's been a long time since I've really rested." Morgan said a little more. He sighed. "I think I'll just rest a while if you don't mind."

"Hang in there, Morgan, helps on the way!" Barry urged, his eyes on the Doctor who was running to help Morgan. He was followed by Tesla and Einstein, both looking like death warmed over.

Al dropped next to Morgan and put a hand on his shoulder. "We're going to get you into the hospital now. You'll be okay, son."

Morgan smiled. "I figured out how the time-lining works, Doc."

"Good, let's talk about it later," Al encouraged him.

Morgan smiled at all his friends and loved ones as they gently lifted him to put him on a stretcher.

"I'll miss you all!" He said, his voice barely above a whisper. He managed to grip Barry and Betty's hands, then pressed them tight. The pain was no longer gripping him. He felt himself sliding into a pleasant darkness.

The last thing he uttered before his last breath was, "I love you so much." Then he let out a long sigh and passed into the stars he had once feared.

Barry howled at the ceiling of the bunker, his frustration and anger and loss erupting like a volcano.

Al took Betty in his arms and held her as she sobbed.

Not a single dry face was there at that moment.

Not one!

Passing of the Baton

Nurse Betty cried against Barry's shoulder as Morgan's body was marched past in a coffin. He was wearing his Sky Captain suit.

No one dared to argue with Einstein and Tesla about the loss of the suit now. They knew that work was done with the man who had worn it.

The Marines carrying the coffin marched to an open grave and then set it down.

They stepped back.

It was dark night.

Any earlier and the Nazis might discover them. But they were still going to honor the man with the best they could.

Al and Tesla marched forward with an American flag and draped it over Morgan's body. Barry put a hand on Morgan's chest; he could barely contain his grief, but he held it together somehow.

He closed the casket.

The casket was lowered into the grave.

Not a single sound was heard at that moment.

Everyone at the base was present. Morgan had been liked and loved by everyone. He was always the kindest person to all of them. And his bravery was beyond reproach. It would go down in history.

No one wanted to give away their position with so many exposed like they were, but tonight they were taking that chance. Even the grunts who manned the anti-aircraft artillery were there, hats over their hearts.

Barry looked around the somber scenario, noting that there wasn't a dry eye there. It was hard to see them clearly though, because his own eyes were blurred with tears. Betty shrieked again in anguish, wrenching at his chest. He held her closer. She needed the comfort of his arms now. Now that...

"Morgan!" Barry whispered as the body was lowered into the grave.

"I will always remember you, pal!" He said a bit more loudly.

Al stepped before the grave when Morgan's body was deposited, opened a small journal to read from. "I was going to make up something wise and spiritual to read to you. Maybe a piece from the old bible, but when I found this and read it, I thought it said everything.

He began to read. "I am really going to miss having all my friends and family of friends around me when my time comes to go into the Big Beyond with that Giant Palooka in the sky. I just hope that when the time comes, you'll all forgive me for the stupid jokes and tacky remarks I made sometimes...well actually..." Al looks up. "...That was Barry who did that, but I feel somehow responsible for the monster I created."

Barry broke into sobs and shook his head.

Al continued. "I want you all to know that no matter what happens. To keep fighting the good fight. There are people out there depending on us. I love you all, you jerks! Morgan!"

The ceremony was deathly silent for several minutes, and then everyone began working their way back to the entrance of the bunker.

Barry and Betty were the last to leave.

Barry suddenly whirled around, grabbing for his sidearm. "Did you hear that?"

Betty gave him a scared look. "What?"

"Like someone laughing."

Barry listened, but heard nothing more. Finally, he took Betty's arm and they headed back into the bunker, whose huge doors silently closed.

A man stood in the shadows of the nearby trees. He watched them enter the bunker, and then stepped out to look at the fresh grave of Morgan and the Sky Captain suit. He grinned. "So that's what it's going to be like, huh God. You finally answer my question. Now can you at least let me go home now so I can share the answer?"

He shook his head as he walked away to the edge of a huge drop off. He adjusted the controls on his chest. The suit began to warm up again.

"Sky Captain is dead. Long live Sky Captain."

He dove off the cliff's edge.

He shot downwards faster and faster as his suit began to vibrate. So much that he could feel it through his bones.

The Sky Captain suit fired, and he shot out of the steep dive and swept upwards.

More work to do yet.

Maybe the next timeline he could get Al to listen to what he'd learned. Maybe then they could put a stop to all this craziness.

He couldn't stay here now. God had other plans for him obviously. He had begun to see stars again as he watched his burial, but once his duplicate was buried; it eased off enough so he could leave safely.

He put on a burst of speed.

"Just call me...Sky Captain!" He screamed as his suit and he shot upwards.

Several night owls screeched in alarm as Sky Captain soared into the atmosphere, leaving a freakish light show behind it as it lifted higher and higher.

The man laying dead in the grave didn't see his duplicate leave, but his soul dead.

And one other.

Barry stood at the entrance to the bunker and saluted to the star rising in the skies.

"So long, pal. We'll meet again!"

Then he shut the door.

DIE TWICE

Deadly Encounter

Harry bit his lower lip as he bore down on the Messerschmitt ME 410s that were arrowing like lethal sharks of the air riding waves of cloud silently below him, stealth their friend as they would not be seen until they broke cover.

Even a sharp lookout's eye wouldn't see them through the haze over the ocean and the clouds barging into each other and shuffling for supremacy in the overly bright skies.

Harry angled slightly to get a better look towards the Allied Forces convoy below. Five freighters, lightly guarded by a single destroyer, American, were making their way across the English channel from France. London was in dire shape after five nights of endless bombings by the Nazi war machine. The buzz bombs, drones that flew like planes, but had rocket engines kept spilling out of the war-torn skies, bursting, breaking, and shattering one building after another, leaving a trail of blood and tears, hemorrhaging fires, and destruction behind them.

Building after building were shook, shattered, and fell victim to ravaging flames that little could be done about because of the ongoing bombing, which would have killed anyone on the streets.

The Brits were going through hell on earth, or as much of one as any country could experience and remain standing.

Sweat accumulated on his eyebrows and upper lip, irritating the hell out of him, but with no visible way to reach and wipe it off, he had to be content with making life as miserable for the unsuspecting Messerschmitt ME 410s as he was about to at that moment.

The rocket suit he wore was heavy, awkward as hell, and felt more like a diving suit than an aerial one, which should have been much more aerodynamic, but what it lost in bulk, it gained in power. Einstein's power pack, which he and Tesla, had secretly developed under Allied support, was powerful enough to blow up half of London were it to detonate. This was another reason why he was sweating.

He wondered briefly what it would feel like to be blown into your component atoms and parts.

Too much science for him at that moment, he concentrated his firepower and his brain on the leading fighter below. It had a bright red swastika smeared over the top of both wings, giving him a clear bull's-eye for what he intended. He only needed to shear off one wing to end their flight and thus their attack.

"All right, Hairy." He told himself. "Time to get your crap together."

He dove like an angry swarm of bees, firing his backpack machine guns as he shot above the flight of Nazi warplanes. They never knew what hit them, until their right or left wings were severed by the attack, and they tumbled side over end to the rough waters below, where they exploded into shrapnel that lit up the night skies.

Thinking it was all over, he put on a burst of speed.

Satisfied he had taken them all out, he shot skywards once more. He never remained in radar reach because he didn't want to give the, by now, confused Nazis any hope or glimmer of hope of following, tracking, or pinning him down. His suit was powerful, but tactics wins any day over power which is led by brutal and stupid movements.

"Harry." His earpiece hammered against his head.

"Softer."

"Sorry, pal."

"Accepted." He shot back with a grin.

"What's your heading?"

"Home."

"Not yet."

Harry swiped at his face, slamming a heavily armored hand against his face piece. His head rang from the blow. He kept forgetting sometimes he wasn't in his old Sky Captain suit he could just strap on his back anymore. No. He was in this enormous monstrosity that looked like a golem from one of the old Jewish monster tales. That's how normal it had begun to feel to him to fly in it. Like it was a second skin now. Albeit a very, very thick one.

Once the ringing in his ears, literally and otherwise, had stopped, Harry asked the Big Question. "Why?"

"Ours is not to question why; ours is but to do and die." Barry shot back, while Harry mouthed it along with him, echoing his buddy. His grin returned once more to his face.

"Then where?"

"Co-ordinates feeding...in one, two...now." Barry announced.

Harry glanced at the tiny screen that was embedded just above his eyeline. He read the co-ordinates and then whistled loudly.

"I hope that wasn't your version of a love tune, Harry, or I'm a dead man."

"Fat chance of that, you gorgeous hunk of man meat." Harry quipped.

Barry chuckled. "That's what I love about you, pal. You know when to bow down to your gods. See ya!"

"Roger that, you sore sack of crap!"

Barry's laugh burst out, then went static and then silent.

Harry swept his arms back to allow for greater air speed, chucked the speed lever with his chin and shot away like a comet across the skies.

Below, sailors were pointing up into the sky where a falling star was streaking across the skies, going faster and faster towards the horizon. The Ship's Captain, watching from the wheel, accidentally had left his radio on. He was the only one of the personnel who knew who and what Harry was. He glanced towards the smoking ruins of the destroyed Nazi air patrol. "Thanks, Harry." He muttered. "God be with you!"

Harry laughed. He was on the same radio frequency. "Sorry. Not room enough." He quipped.

As Harry headed back to America, he thought about the co-ordinates again. No one was supposed to know those, but Barry had broadcast them on an open channel. Why?

Harry was nearing the islands of Hawaii when a shadow edged slowly past his outstretched arms.

He gave his suit a quick roll over, flying upside down, and saw the gigantic form of a Nazi V Bomber. They were stealth and meant to fly at high altitudes. They were also experimental and supposed to be only theoretical, not built. Someone had gotten bad Intel and he was about to pay for it. But no rockets. No machine gun bursts arrowed in on him, tracking the sky with their deadly, fatal bites of destruction.

That was odd. Could this be why Barry had sent him to these co-ordinates?

He leveled off again and swept his arms forward, causing the internals in his suit to follow his movements and as he raised his arms, the suit followed. He gave his chin a shove to the accelerator below it, leveraging it rapidly. As he did the suit put on a burst of speed. He grunted as the gees struck him.

Einstein had said the problem was fixed, but only a bit. He still felt like a worm plastered against a brick wall when he gave it everything it had. But if he didn't give it everything he had, he would be more than just a worm against a wall, and he'd be dead.

He closed in on the massive bomber. As he did, its glistening copper colors began to hurt his vision. He slipped his sun-visor over his helmet and was able to focus better.

It had tri wings. Three levels of wings that could move in and out of the body of the main fuselage. The uppermost wing was as large as two football fields, the second half as large, and the last again half as much. He knew from what Einstein and Tesla had told him, that each configuration allowed better performance than the last.

Right now, it had all three wings deployed, which would play hell with any radar lucky enough to be focused in his direction. He also noticed that a steady stream of silver slipped out the nose of the craft, silvering the sky with debris so tiny only a microscope, or a magnified vision like his, could spot it.

It was in effect totally invisible to the ground and the air unless one happened to be on the same course or looking up when it passed over.

Its nose was painted to look like a demon's mouth, with sharp razor teeth and eyes that glowed bloody red. In German on its right fuselage side were the words, "Hell freezes over!"

Indeed.

"Closing on V Bomber."

"A V what?" Barry shot back, sounding perplexed by the announcement.

"Stealth bomber, Barry. The kind that's strictly paper."

"You telling me you're scouting a paper bomber?"

"No, idiot, I'm telling you the paper bomber is now the real thing. You've got to let command now immediately. Its headings are..."

Harry looked at the co-ordinates on his screen, and then felt a wave of terror roll over him. He almost lost control of the suit for a moment, and it began to plummet like a stone. He caught himself and nudged the controls steady once more. His arms swept upwards, and he pushed to close the distance.

"It's faster than me." Harry hollered.

"Damn! Where's it heading?"

"Let's just say that our friends in America are about to get a friendly visit from the smiling mortician." Harry joked, even as he felt sick to his stomach.

"I don't have any friends in America."

"Won't matter much if you do now."

"Why?"

"It's got atomics strapped to its belly."

Barry sputtered on the other end. Harry could hear him hollering for Al and Nick, his names for Einstein and Tesla.

"Describe them." Barry shot back finally.

Harry could hear Tesla and Einstein hollering questions at him.

The command post must be in full riot mode by now, knowing what was coming.

"Size of a wingless Messerschmitt. Silver tips. Arrow feather tails."

"Shit!" Barry cursed.

"Barry, watch your mouth." Harry joked.

"You mean wipe my mouth, because all kinds of crap are about to come out of it."

"What's going on?"

"Evac. Harry, we gotta go. We got a lock on to the V. It's heading right for us. We only have a few hours to lock down and get the hell outta here."

"Where to?"

Barry laughed. "Wouldn't you like to know?"

Harry chuckled. He had just acknowledged the code. Now, would he be able to get to that bastard above him before it carved a chunk of America into radioactive carbon bits?

Malfunction

The worst part of being a grunt, a swabby, or a flyboy was that you never got a day off. The worst part was also that you never got a night off either. So, it was equally as unfair to both parts of your life. Like a Dagwood sandwich, with you in between the slices of bread.

Funny philosophy, but it worked. If hell could eat you for breakfast, it was just as invited for dinner. No main course without dessert.

Harry sat with his back against a palm tree, watching the waves roll onto shore, bright sparkling clouds of blue water that curled inwards and then flew upwards and smashed down on the wet sands, until it relented in its attack and withdrew for another attempt, leaving draining fingers of wet sand behind its withdrawal. His eyes were half closed. His head felt like a broken anvil. His landing hadn't gone so well. At the last possible moment his jet pack had malfunctioned. He had survived the crash, but he would have a headache for the rest of his life probably.

He glanced at the bruised and dented rocket suit he had discarded and dragged into the thick tropical brush.

He hadn't destroyed the bomber like he had hoped. It had some new kind of technology that killed his shoulder pack missiles. So, he had done the only reasonable thing possible. He had used his rocket suit to bust up its aerial controls.

As he rammed through the aerial controls aboard the massive bomber, every single circuit in his rocket suit lit up like Christmas on the Fourth of July. The bomber had exploded, enveloping him and his Sky Captain suit in a ball of hellfire ten times hotter than the surface of the sun. He blanked out for a moment of time. When he recovered his senses, he was plummeting like a rock. A very, very heavy one towards the Pacific below.

At the very last moment he came back to his senses. He had time to level out and smash into the beach of an island off Hawaii. He didn't know which one, all his interior equipment was on the fritz. All he knew was that he might be in his own time stream or another. He remembered the bomber exploding and then he lost consciousness. But as he was enveloped in the darkness, he felt his body altering in some way. It reminded him of the zone of entropy he had run into the last time he had altered time realities. He prayed it hadn't done so again. But he had no way of knowing for sure. His communications gear and his scanning equipment were all dead to the world.

He winced as he tried to get more comfortable again. The sun was baking him, but the moist salt air was renewing and reviving him. Now if only every single damn muscle and his bone would stop hurting!

He must have fallen asleep, because when his eyes opened again, he saw a huge moon hovering higher overhead. It caused the beach to glow like a magical playground. He spotted several sea turtles crawling slowly up the beach from the surf, trailing paths of glistening silver from the water pouring off their backs.

He watched them crawl far enough inland to escape the high and low tides of the ocean, and then began digging, slowly, but steadily. They were majestic and beautiful. He loved turtles. He had a box turtle when he was a kid and had watched it grow from a tiny thing, he could hold in his hands to one he could ride on its back. Boxy. Boxy he had named it. He smiled, remembering those more innocent times.

Oh well, he sighed to himself.

His battered body could stay awake no longer and the warmth of the sun was sapping what little strength he had left. He began to drift off. As he did, he could have sworn he saw himself standing in front of him in this weird looking outfit, a sad look on his face and then he slipped into the deeper realms of sleep.

Not even the sound of the loud sea gulls pluming across the beach and pecking for food, or the incessant drumming sound of the surf slamming on the beach stirred him. Had they done so, he might have seen the blossoms of light in the distance. Huge blossoms of light that resembled mushroom clouds.

Sky Captain Tech

"Damn it, Harry!" Barry screamed at him. "Don't you go getting all time lost on me again!"

Harry jerked up on his bed, rubbing at his eyes. He was just dreaming was all. He gave Barry a sour look. "A man needs his beauty rest."

"Yeah. Like that would really help an ugly mutt like you." Barry grumped, then strode from the room they shared together.

Harry didn't see the smile on Barry's face.

Another day. Another day. He thought, as he stretched again, and then rose to do a quick shower. The new Sky Captain suit was getting hydraulic repairs and he wanted to be in on it, even if he wasn't the greatest of mechanics like Barry, he needed to at least have enough understanding to fix something if he ever got into a little bit of a jam. At least enough to save his butt. This happened more and more these days since he had taken on the mantle of the Sky Captain.

Sky Captain. He mused as he twirled the hot water knob of the shower, drowning his body in steamy, hot water. It felt like a million fingers pounding his sore flesh. He had been exercising heavily the last several weeks to toughen up for his next mission.

Those made him think about Sky Captain again. What had once been an experimental suit he had worn during the end of World War Two had become now, instead, a huge device taller than his own six foot plus frame and weighing about half a ton. It was a tank missile driving its rider through the air like a rocket, pounding the flesh, shaking the soul. He smiled. Shaken, but not stirred. *Where had he heard that before?*

Sky Captain Harry Jackson, hero of World War Two. Knocker of Messerschmitt heads together times twenty. Highly decorated. Frequently wounded, and usually so tired he could sleep a thousand years. Able to fly into space...scary that...and plunge into the depths of the ocean in a blink. A suit with the power of a submarine, a rocket, a jet, and a tank, as well as a killing machine...all built into one handy helluva huge piece of metal and advanced technology that only the likes of Tesla and Einstein could understand.

He had come close to saving the world at the end of World War Two...in one timeline...only to have it won by the Nazis...in another...and wake up from the near dead in a frozen lake off the Alps of Switzerland, then gifted by timeline variations of Einstein and Tesla with the suit he was going to fly today. Sky Captain. Hero and Savior.

He broke into laughter.

"I hear you, Harry!" Barry hollered into the bathroom. "Don't you go getting all mental on me!"

He ignored his friend, who was obviously worried to death about him. *Hell! He was worried to death about himself.* He turned up the hot water several more notches and luxuriated in the fresh floods of hot steam, fresh from the flash warmed water tanks below the base that Tesla had fixed up for everyone. It used the new power system, as did most of their equipment; to draw energy from something he called Quark Matter. Or was it Dark Matter? Didn't matter. It worked. And did it ever.

He jumped out of the shower before he turned into a red lobster, began slapping his back and legs with a fresh white towel that was beginning to show some wear and tear, like most of his friends clothing and wearable's. Nothing new coming in from the Americas anymore since the Nazis had blockaded it with their force screens.

Even though he could evade them with his newly altered suit, it was a shut down and eat the dirt scenario for all the other Americans and Europeans caught outside the domes of energy. Anything touching them...flesh or metal...were instantly melted or barbecued.

He threw some deodorant under his arms and some baby powder in his shorts, and then slapped his face with some aftershave, even if he wasn't shaving. He had a facial growth sprouting now that made him look like one of those criminals that used to be in the movies with Gene Autry and Roy Rogers. Evil villains. Ha-ha. He laughed silently.

He almost ran from his quarters. He flashed a quick look at his pocket watch and almost knocked down Al, who had been heading the same way from a different direction...the labs...where he and Nicolas put together their works of madness...not his words, but that of his grunt buddies, the forces that guarded the base on land.

"Whoa, son, where's the bomb going off?" Al teased him, his wild hair flaring above his eyebrows, complimenting his head of hair which made him look like the Bride of Frankenstein from one of those old horror movies.

"Sorry, Pops!" He teased back.

Al grinned and slapped him on the back. "C'mon, they're just about ready to install the new hydraulics. Wouldn't want to miss out on the new craziness, would we?"

"Bet your life I wouldn't." He responded happily.

He and Al were like father and son, even though Al was only twice his age, but looked only half of that. The man never seemed to age. Everyone told him that. He had asked Al once and he had given him a big grin. "Law of Relativity, dear boy. Law of Relativity."

"Now what in the hell does that mean?" He had immediately asked.

Al had just winked, laughed, and walked away.

They passed the main hanger floor, where the secret squadrons of planes were hangered, waiting for the secret missions they flew on a regular basis...to harass and destroy as much of the Nazi War Machine as possible.

They were brave men and usually outnumbered, but most of them came back. He slowed as they passed the planes and then crossed himself when he saw the embedded plaques in the floor with names on them.

Al stopped beside him. "They were good men. Great pilots. They shall be missed."

Harry had nodded. He knew his own name was as likely to face one of those plaques soon. Only a lot of luck and some right moves had proven otherwise. But Mother Death was waiting to take him home in her arms. Every man on the basis believed they had a ticket; they just didn't know when it was going to be collected.

"Ah, here we are." Al said as they rounded the last plane and saw the Sky Captain suit raised on the street framework on which it was being repaired. Barry was overseeing the work. His hand was in everything that touched the suit. He had even made some modifications to it that surprised both Nick and Al, causing them both to watch him more closely.

Tesla had even started giving his best friend private lessons in the Mechanics of the Universe as he called them.

When Harry had asked Al about it, his eyes had twinkled, and he had stuck out his tongue in disgust. "The man is a charlatan. All he is about is fireworks and more fireworks."

"Yeah. Fireworks that help me kick the vanilla asses of the Nazis!" Harry added.

"Yes. And that too." Ad admitted with his usual grin of dismissal.

"Hey!" Barry greeted as Harry arrived, hands in his pockets. He was nervous about the work as usual and didn't want Barry to see his hands shaking. But Barry knew him only too well.

"Cool your jets, man." He told Harry. "Everything's under control."

He touched a remote in his hand and the Rocket suit stepped down from the framework on its own, causing the engineers and techs working on it to scramble to safety as it raised its arms to battle stance, like a kung fu robot, raising one arm upwards and the other out, and planting both feet firmly apart on the hardened floor.

"Impressive." Harry admitted. "But can it cook?"

Barry gave Harry a big grin. "Oh, can it ever."

The Sky Captain suit jerked as a barrage of tiny missiles launched from the outreaching fist and slammed into a makeshift target with a small bull's eye in its center. Every single one of the missiles struck the center, causing the target to shatter like broken glass. The expended missiles collapsed to the floor and rolled in numerous directions.

Barry looked about him and all the crew that had dove for cover, including Harry and Al. "Uh, it's not what you think, guys. They're not loaded with explosives."

Everyone started to get up when one of the missiles exploded.

Time Clone

Barry and Harry entered the commissary eating area and as they did people glanced their way. Some giving Barry nasty looks. Others rolling their eyes.

"Hey!" Barry finally hollered. "I'm not the man responsible for giving me a loaded dummy!"

The cafeteria went stone quiet for a moment, and then everyone burst into laughter.

Barry scowled and hurried along the chow line, tossing food onto his plate without caring what it was. Finished, he sat as far away from everyone as he could. Harry took his time, selecting pot roast, potatoes, asparagus, strawberries and cream and a huge mug of java, which he loaded with sugar until it seemed that's all he could see in the cup.

He slid his tray onto Barry's table and shrugged into a chair opposite him.

"Have some coffee in your sugar, man." Barry said.

"Don't mind if I do." Harry said with a grin.

Barry finally let out a blast of air and relaxed. "I'm sorry. I'm just pissed off that the dummy went live on me. I double checked them. I swear I did."

Harry grew very serious. "How serious?"

"Like five times. Hey, man, you know I would never hurt a fly if I didn't have too." He said, as he swatted a fly seated on the table edge, preening itself.

He looked up at Harry, who was watching him solemnly.

"Hey!" Barry growled.

Harry barked with laughter.

"Look, Barry, the stress is getting to all of us. We're like dead men walking."

"You don't mean Zombies, do you, Harry? I hate those things." Barry complained. "My mother used to tell me bedtime stories about Voodoo doctors and Zombies who got little kids who didn't do their homework."

Barry sighed, took a fist full of bread and began nibbling on it. "Where's that damned butter when you need it?"

"Probably in some Nazi Commander's pantry." Harry offered.

"Yeah. There's that." Barry admitted.

He looked up. "It worked. I learned well. Real well."

"And the end result being...?" Harry asked, munching on his pot roast that he had draped over an asparagus like a sandwich.

"Uh. I guess it made me the man I am now. In the end I became good at anything I tried. Except for saving my mother." He said, sadness suffusing his face then.

Harry reached a hand out and put it on Barry's arm. "Pal, she's loving you to death wherever she is now. I just know it."

Barry gave Harry a look of gratitude and went back to nibbling on his bread. Finally, he threw it down, got up and stormed off, a hand over his eyes. He hated letting people see his weakness.

"Hey flyboy. Mind if a cute nursey puts in her two cents?" Harriet asked, dropping into the chair next to Harry without waiting for an answer.

She crossed her shapely right leg over her other leg and brushed them both a moment, as if reminding herself there were no stockings on them, then straightened up to look at Harry, whose eyes had been following the movements.

"Men have died for less." She told him with a smirk.

"And loved it every minute of their death." He replied with a grin.

She leaned over and gave him a gentle hug. "You worry me, flyboy. Too much flying. No crying and no lying."

He gave her a lusty grin. "Oh, I could go for some of that jazz, but..."

She smiled and patted his hands. "You just go on thinking that, Harry. Just go on thanking that."

"Mind if I join you two love birds?" Nicolas Tesla asked, sitting down opposite Harriet, and setting two cups of coffee down. One in front of him and one her. She gave him a warm look.

"If I were ten years older, you'd be in trouble, Nicky."

"If I were ten years younger, I'd already be in trouble." He replied, a laughing glance of his eyes taking her in. "But I think my wife might have something to say about both of those possibilities."

"Not to mention, Al." Harry quipped. "He's already proposed to her twice."

"Ten times." Harriet corrected.

Both Nicky and Harry gave her surprised looks. "After all he isn't married to his job like you boys, or a wife."

She got up, yawned, and shoved her chair into the table. "It's late. It's late and I've got a very important date."

Harry gave her a hurt look. She bent down and brushed her lips across his forehead, leaving a red track of lipstick there. "Don't go letting those ideas go burning holes in your head, Rocket boy, my dates with a mattress and two pillows." She laughed and walked off.

"I love her." Nicky said.

Harry nodded. "Guess that makes four."

Nicky looked at him.

"Barry and Al too."

Nicky laughed.

His laughter vanished when sirens broke out.

Then a blinding light flared. So intense he thought the very sun itself had exploded in his face.

Choking on Sea Bottom

"Harry."

Tranquility and darkness.

"Harry, wake up."

No more tranquility and darkness.

Wetness.

Choking.

Harry struggled to open his eyes, and when he did, he saw they were under water. Inside his helmet. He began frantically trying to get out of the water, but it was too deep. Then he relaxed a bit, even as his lungs began to feel as if they might explode from lack of oxygen.

The Sky Captain suit had crashed into the ocean waters.

He was on the floor. Damn!

He slowly looked up. He could see light.

He looked down.

His feet were wedged between two shelves of coral reef.

He struggled to break free.

His oxygen was running out.

He was running out of options.

He lowered his arm and carefully aimed.

Another Life

The fishermen were casting their nets from the sandy beach, wearing nothing at all, allowing the sun to tan their already bronzed bodies further. No shame at their nakedness existed. Why should it? They had nothing to hide. No needs to compare or compete. They were humble fishermen. They needed food for their families. That's all that mattered. Putting food on the table.

And it was warm. Very warm.

Even the surf was warm. Probably not less than body temperature, so the water flowing and ebbing about their legs felt as soothing as a bath might to us, and no more dangerous.

"There!" Pointed one. A tall fellow with long black locks. His eyes were hazel brown, and he had a scar on his right shoulder from a fall he took as a child. It had never quite healed properly, but a friendly American had landed with several funny men in black and white who claimed to carry God in their books.

They had secretly laughed at the men who called themselves the Messengers of God and had admired the American who humbly and simply set about healing all those in their village. Never asking for a thing. Claiming a single thing.

If there were any truth to their God, then it was in this man, named Harry.

No one knew where he had come from. He was tall and powerfully built. He seemed to know many things about the West and about war, which troubled them, but he never spoke of the war except when the strange flashes flared on the horizon of the ocean, and then he would remember briefly, but only briefly that he had once been a warrior.

The tall fellow, whose name was Loche, lowered his hand. The school of fish he had spotted in the crystal-clear waters had been spooked by something. Very strange. They were seldom frightened so easily. Often, they would even come up to his on hand to take the bait, as if willingly offering up their bodies for consumption.

He and his fellow tribesmen never took advantage of the fish. They thanked them for their sacrifice and never took more than they needed.

The waters suddenly exploded upwards in a huge geyser of steam and smoke.

The fishermen all fell back from the raging waters, muttering fearfully and doing the peculiar crossing of the heart the Messengers of God had taught them, as well as spitting on the ground and grinding their foot into the spit. Supposedly this warded off all evil spirits.

And today they needed to do so.

Coming out of the geyser of steam and smoke and surging waters was a tall figure, almost eight feet tall. A God!

They cried out in alarm.

There was a God. And he had come to punish them for chasing his Messengers off their lovely island.

But no one ran. They were too simple to run. They had no reason to fear this God. Yet. It offered no harm to them. It just stood in the raging geyser, as if floating on a bubble of air, then it began striding onto the land.

It reached the beach, and then froze.

The head of the creature made an odd sound and then began to turn in a circle. Slowly, then faster.

The men were in terror then. What manner of being could turn its head like that and not die?

Then the head fell off and water sloshed out and Harry. Or what looked like Harry. His head floated at the top of the odd man and made choking sounds.

"Help!" He cried out.

The odd creature fell towards them. Everyone ran screaming away, thinking it was attacking them.

All but Loche.

He had heard the word, "Help!" He understood it. The American Harry had taught him English or American English as he called it.

Angels of Death

Harry woke up in a bamboo hut, woven together with palm fronds. He lay on a mat woven from fronds and grass. The sweet scent of coconuts wafted in the air. He felt something stroking his chest and that startled him the rest of the way to consciousness. He was lying naked on the mat and a beautiful woman in her late forties was applying a salve across his bruised body made of coconuts.

She gave him a bright smile. "Wake?"

She pressed him gently back down on the mat from his startled position and he relaxed. Her touch was like magic. He could feel the oil soaking into his bruised muscles. She tilted an open coconut half to his mouth, and he drank. Coconut juice.

"Good!" She said, nodding her head.

He tried to nod but groaned instead.

A worried look touched her sweet face. "Not good?"

He touched her arm gently. "Good." Touched his neck. "Sore. Very, very sore."

"Ah." She nodded. "Good and sore."

He laughed.

His laughter released a lot of tension that had built up within him over the last forty-eight hours. Then he felt sleep stealing over him. He relaxed into it and drifted off into visions of mushroom clouds and flying men.

He saw children pointing at them fearfully. "Angels of death!"

Then he fell into a deep, dark sleep with no more dreams.

Healing

Harry fell in and out of sleep and strange dreams for the next two weeks. Later he would learn that his body had bruises over every inch of it. Must have been from the non-powered landing he had been forced to make. He had struck the water at over twice the speed of sound and smashed into the coral reefs offshore. He was lucky to be alive. The meal of his rocket suit had protected him from overt breaking of his bones, but the padding inside wasn't meant to absorb a direct blow like he had taken in the air when the German V Bomber had nuked him.

Yes. He remembered it all now. Clear as a diamond. He had been closing in on the V Bomber, knowing it was heading directly for New York City. The Defense Alliance had broken down the Nazi Overlords who had taken it some twenty years back and established an energy dome to protect it from further incursions by the Nazi Warlords, but Hitler's minions were nothing if not persistent when it came to dealing death and destruction. Even the vast power of the energy dome couldn't withstand the direct blow of a Cobalt Bomb...the massive successor to an atomic bomb and the weapon that had overthrown Western Civilization in the last days of World War Two, and thus ensuring that freedom had been reduced to struggling bands of resistance fighters.

It had taken them decades to forge an alliance and build their secret base in the Alps, and his discovery by the granddaughter of the woman whom he had loved many years before, retrieving him from the deep sleep that his friends had devised for him inside his Sky Captain suit if he was ever disabled. It had worked. Worked better than intended. He had landed in a glacier that had quickly frozen over and the combination of the deep freeze and the sleep drugs his body had been injected with automatically sustained him for the decades that were to follow.

When Hillary had first discovered him, she had been amazed when he had awoken and cracked a stupid American joke at the time. "How many Nazis does it take to screw in a lightbulb?" He had asked her.

"Every one of them." She had replied.

"Nope." He had pointed out. "One to grab the light bulb and the rest to turn him."

He had laughed so hard; he had started to hemorrhage his lungs. Only her quick thinking and medical skills, and that of her mother had spared him a deep and lasting death. Which, later, he had wished for once he learned how many decades had elapsed since he had gone into the artificial coma.

To wake up a hundred years later and find out you haven't aged one day and everyone you ever knew and loved was gone. Well, it was heart wrenching at best. Lethal at its worst.

Hillary had nursed him through the worst of it. Even once climbing into his bed with him and holding him close, whispering words of love that his lost love had once spoken to him.

And that's when he finally began to let go of the past. It took almost a year and hard physical retraining of his body, to rebuild the muscles, to strengthen his stamina once more and light up his sluggish mind. During that period, she and her mother, the grandmother of his original girlfriend had nursed and cared for him fastidiously, allowing no one to intrude on his peace of mind.

He grinned. No one except for Al, of course. That rascal genius had been so curious about him once he heard about him that he had immediately sought him out and began drilling him about what the world war had been like and his alternate self.

Yes, alternate self. It seems, adding even further alienation to Harry's life situation, that when he had been caught in the nuclear blast of Nazi's Super Troopers, that his suit's unusual power supply had somehow been transformed in such a way that he had been separated from his original time stream into one of many.

Many, because he fell in and out of multiple alternate realities. Never planned. Never expected and always challenging. He had found friends and lovers in all of them and one enemy who seemed to stretch across all the time zones. Hitler!

War

"War?" Loche had asked, puzzled by Harry's urgency. "What war?"

Harry tried for what must have been the hundredth time to get the man to understand that he had to get back to battling the Nazi War Machine. The Defense Alliance needed his skills and expertise.

Loche had finally shaken his head. "No Nazi War Machine here."

With those final words, he had risen and left a very stunned Harry to ponder the meaning of what had happened to him. Had he been thrown into yet another alternate timeline or was this island so removed from the violence going on around the world, that no one had a clue of the horrors surrounding them.

He had wandered the beach that night, dressed only in shorts woven from palm leaves and grass. He was barefoot. It was then he saw her.

She rose from the silvered surf waters of the ocean like an ancient sea goddess, wringing her hair dry of the salt and water as she stepped lightly onto the beach. He was so stunned, that he stopped, with his mouth hung open.

She was stark naked. As were all the people of the tribe he had been lucky enough to have been saved by. And there wasn't a part of her bronzed golden beauty that lacked. She was perfection in motion. She was the poetry of beauty and grace. She was...

"Ilyana." She told him, touching her right breast suggestively with a demure smile, as if aware of his interest, but still unsure what else might be going on in his mind.

"You?" She pointed, touching his left breast.

Then he felt this wave of relief flood over him. She wasn't coming onto him at all. It was custom and then he remembered Loche's partner doing the same with Loche. It was a ritual of friendship and acknowledgement.

She began to laugh. She put a hand to her beautiful lips and looked away. "Sorry."

"Not, it's all right." He told her. "I'm just a jerk for staring. I've never seen anyone so beautiful before."

And right then and there he knew he had made a colossal mistake as visions of Hillary and Harriet came into his mind and his passion for them as well.

What a crazy mixed-up life when he didn't know whom to love, and whom to get attached to anymore.

"Harry." He finally managed to stutter, blushing all over at the juvenile idiocy he was displaying at that moment and at the rising of the grass shorts he wore. "Oh damn!" He cursed, and then ran and dived into the surf, leaving her behind.

When he resurfaced, she was still standing there, and watching him.

But now Loche stood by her, smiling.

"Come, Harry." He told him.

Harry tried not to look at Ilyana as he came out of the water. The surf had destroyed his sudden physical interest in the beautiful young woman. He sighed with relief. He hadn't felt that strong about someone since he was a teen.

Loche nodded to him. "Ilyana. My daughter."

Harry groaned. "I... I'm sorry. I didn't mean to..."

Loche laughed. "Harry. Man, not man who not like good woman. But enough of this, we have something to show you. Something you must see and know."

Harry gave Loche a puzzled look.

Ilyana took his right hand and Loche the left.

"Please keep your heart open, Harry. I worry for you." Loche told Harry.

"I'm strong."

"He's strong, Papa. He's crushing my hand."

Harry let go. She laughed and took it back. "Kidding. Joke. No?"

He gave Loche a searching look, but his face was impassive and that worried Harry, but they kept on walking a long time. Finally, Harry was getting a bit exhausted.

"Here, Harry."

Loche pointed to a small cave opening whose roof was built of stone and firmly built to weather the strongest of storms. He was startled when he saw a familiar sight hanging over the entrance.

"My helmet!" He cried out, running to retrieve it. But when he plucked it down, it felt wrong somehow.

Loche came up and shook his head. "Come."

Harry put the helmet back and followed Loche into the cave, with Ilyana in tow behind both. It brightened as they went deeper, as artificial lights came on, revealing a walkway of compressed stone and walls with drawer and cabinets built into them.

"His home once." Loche remarked sadly.

They took a slight turn and Harry almost fainted. The old rocket suit he used to wear in his original timeline. It was hanging on a stone peg, as new looking as if it had never been worn or battle tested. He glanced at Loche. "How is this possible?"

Loche stopped and crossed his arms. "Harry tells me."

Harry looked about the small bedchamber they had entered. He saw a book on a small stand. It was open. The title of the first page was: The Adventures of Sky Captain.

"Damn!" He swore beneath his breath.

A journal of my brief, but very fulfilled life. By Harry Jackson. He read. "Captain Harry Jackson." He read out loud, turning to look at Loche.

"It seems that wise men die twice, Harry." Loche uttered with great passion.

"How?" Harry asked, knowing he couldn't say the word.

"Saving Ilyana." Loche said.

Ilyana wiped at her eyes then, the smile lost to her lips, her face pale and haggard. "We were to be married."

"What happened?" Harry asked.

Magnetic Storm

It was an unusual night. The tenth in a row. Strange magnetic storms were plying the heavens above the island. Loche noted that the grass on the sand was standing straight up, as if a magnet were above them, drawing them upwards. Yet, he knew this was impossible. Harry had told him about magnets, and they only affected iron, like the knife he wore on his hip at times and the tip of his spear he used for fishing.

Then the skies in front of him had opened and a vessel of unseemly proportions, resembling an outrigger with four levels of out-rigging smashed through a tremendous blast of energies. The sea in front of him roared angrily and pulled back. At first, he thought it was one of those rare times when the sea withdrew to come smashing back inland wiping everything out for dozens of yards, but instead it withdrew into this huge angry boiling spout of water.

He began running.

He made it back to their home, calling out for Ilyana, but she didn't hear. He raced inside and shook her awake. She had been tired lately. Though he hadn't known why at the time.

"Come. Danger!" He had told her with no explanation.

None needed.

She had thrown a few things into a vine sack she had made, and then they began running deeper into the island. They hadn't gotten far when the strange sky ship had swept overhead, causing the palm trees to bend over backwards from the force of its passage. It threw them to the ground.

Loche had thought it was just passing by, but it wasn't.

It stopped suddenly.

As they began to climb to their feet a huge light of some kind shot from the bow of the vessel and speared them both in its angry glare, illuminating their bodies like the light of the sun during the day.

That was when things got bad. Really bad.

Huge bursts of something unknown to them began exploding into the ground behind them. Loche spun around, thinking someone was there, but what he saw horrified him. Huge palm trees were being shredded to pieces, like his knife would do to the soft coconut butter before cooking.

"RUN!" He cried out.

"Harry!" She screamed.

"No time!" He told her, barely able to get her to hear him over the thunder of the discharge that was edging towards them in a rain of death.

They began running, but then the forest ahead of them exploded like a nightmare into their faces, hurtling them backwards. Helpless, they lay on the shattered ground as a rain of terror from both directions closed in on them.

Then it happened!

The sky burst into a cataclysm of energies that shattered the forest for miles round and threw them dozens of feet through the air.

Sacrifice

Ilyana burst into sobs that wracked her chest with pain and horror. Loche put his arm about her shoulders and pulled her close, comforting her.

Harry felt their pain. Both had been touched deeply.

Ilyana finally stopped.

Loche let go and motioned to the rocket suit. "He was an angel sent to save us."

Great big tears of grief wet his eyes as he explained. "The invader of our skies was stopped when he struck it with his own body."

Harry gasped. "Then..."

Ilyana looked at him, her eyes glazed with misery. "He died instantly. Mercifully. The man I loved with all my heart. And our baby."

"Baby?"

"Yes." She said, her sadness deepening.

Loche explained. "He sacrificed his life to stop them. He had always said the suit had enough power for one more flight. He never took that flight. Till then."

Harry looked at the old, beaten-up rocket suit and understood then. "I'm sorry." He told them, his heart swelling with respect for the man...himself from another time stream, some alternate reality...who had been the kind of hero he had seen so many times in the war against the bastard Nazis. Sacrificing his own life to protect the life of three others: Loche, Ilyana and their baby.

Harry wondered in his heart of hearts if he could do the same were such ever required of him. He didn't wonder for long as he stared at the beaten suit. He could. He had.

Another World

Harry finished dragging his Sky Captain suit into the cave that Harry had constructed with the help of Ilyana and Loche, who both proved to be equally as strong as himself. They had rigged a makeshift slid from fallen palm fronds and reinforced them with weaves of grass and smaller branches, so it was sturdy enough to take the weight. Gradually and over the next two weeks they had managed to slide the suit to the entrance and then inside, where Loche and Harry, with great effort, managed to stand it.

"It's so big!" Ilyana gasped as it was raised. She hadn't realized before while it was horizontal just how big it was.

She looked at Harry. "You are a giant inside that thing!"

"More like a midget inside that thing." He admitted. Then he slapped the side of it affectionately. "But its home." He frowned. "Or at least it was home."

"Now what?" Loche asked.

Harry shook his head. "I'm not sure yet. Maybe there's some way I can take the best of both suits and get something to work."

"You can do that?" Ilyana gasped in awe.

Harry grinned. "Miracles happen sometimes."

She gave him a sudden hug. "You're just like Harry!"

She suddenly realized what she was doing and pushed back from him, blushing. "I'm sorry. I didn't..." She burst into tears and ran from the cave, sobbing.

Loche stopped Harry from going after her. "No. Let her let go of the pain."

Harry looked at the kindly face. "I feel so terrible for her. For you. He was a good man. I don't know if I can ever measure up to him. What he did. His sacrifice had to have been very great for him.

"To lose all he had planned for, his love, his child. You."

Loche looked away, his eyes seeking another world. "I cared deeply for him. He was a good man."

"You know that if they found this world once, they can find it again. You have to know that." Harry told Loche, even though he hated himself for having to do it the moment Loche cringed as if struck.

Loche smiled bitterly. "Let's pray that never has to happen."

The Long Haul

Harry didn't go back to the home he had shared with Loche and Ilyana, though they returned to visit him every day, watching with curiosity as he began taking apart his newer suit to salvage it for parts to repair the older one. He worked every hour he could force himself to stay awake in.

Ilyana came in, like a ghost, unheard and unseen and brought him food and drink.

Exhausted he had turned to stop her with a touch to her wrist. "I haven't thanked you enough for your help."

She gave him a grateful smile, then broke his grip and almost ran from the cave.

Harry sighed. "Damn! I just can't do anything right these days."

"Don't be so hard on yourself, Harry." Loche said.

Harry turned around, startled. He hadn't heard the man enter. "Scared the crap outta me."

Loche frowned. "Another Americanism?"

Harry grinned. "Yeah. Big one. And we get lots of practice with that one these days. Not only in my original timeline, but a few more besides."

Loche sat down and crossed one leg over another in a yogi style position. He leaned forward. "You will not break her heart."

Harry was about to unscrew a piece of his suit and accidentally stabbed himself instead with the emergency screwdriver that was kitted aboard his larger suit.

"Ow! Damnit to hell!" He cried out and jumped up, cursing to himself as blood sprouted in beads from the puncture he had made.

Harry finally settled down, when Loche handed him a piece of leaf to place over the wound. "It will close the wound and stop any infection."

"Too bad it doesn't work on foul mouths too." Harry quipped.

Loche grinned at him. "If it did that, how would any of us ever be able to open our mouths again?"

Harry laughed. "Good point, pal."

He dropped back next to his rocket suit, retrieved his emergency screwdriver, and put it to the screw in his suit with his other hand, wincing as his wounded hand accidentally brushed the edge of one of the arms. "Crap!"

Loche burst into laughter.

Things Happen

Harry wiped a dirty hand across his brow, eyed his handiwork and then set the older suit back onto its hanger. He dusted himself off as best he could, and then set down his tools in a corner on the makeshift stand he had built for them. Satisfied, he exited the cave and headed for the beach. It didn't take too long; the cave was close.

He settled down between two rises of sand, allowing the surf to crash upwards and slide warmly over his exposed feet. He didn't bother dressing up much anymore. *Not that he could*, he laughed to himself.

He sat there a long time, watching the sun begin to settle on the horizon. As he did, he felt a presence behind him. He smiled.

"You walk like an angel." He told her.

Ilyana sat next to him and smiled. "I thought Angels had wings. Like you!"

He looked into her eyes. Oh damn! He thought to himself. I can't. I can't. I just...

She took the decision from him and leaned forward and pressed her lips to his mouth. He almost pulled back, but something told him to not do it and he allowed himself to savor the kiss. It lasted a long time. He felt this heady energy, like he had just packed his nervous system with a jug of high caffeine java.

When she finally pulled back, her eyes were smiling, though her face was sad.

He touched her lightly on the cheek. "We shouldn't do this. You know this can't last."

"Does anything?" She asked, the smile in her eyes finally reaching her cheeks and lips.

He looked down at his feet, which were getting caressed by the descending surf water as the waters receding back into the ocean before their next rush up the sandy slopes of the beach to grab for his feet once more.

He sighed. "Where I come from, men and women..." He stopped and eyed her sidewise, his face tilted slightly. "...they make promises."

"As in our world, Harry." She replied.

"But they can't always keep them. Things happen."

"War." She announced bitterly. "Man's war against himself."

He was startled by both the vehemence and the clarity of her reply and insight. "You've thought about it a lot, haven't you...the old...?"

"Harry?" She asked. Nodded. "We spent hours talking about...war. Peace. War. Peace. How men and women turned against each other. Brother against brother. Man against wife."

"It must have made you sad. Your world seems so...."

"Simple?" She asked him with a slight smile. "Hardly. It only appears that way. You see Loche has not told you everything about why we are here." She gestured to the island. "This lonely place."

He waited expectantly for her to explain. She did.

"Father was in the military before we came here. I was still a child of ten at the time. But he was a good father. A good man. I remember him giving speeches in the halls of our town, pleading with the leaders of the nation to use reason and love, not logic and hate."

She looked down. Sadness on her face. "He failed. He was honorable. He fought for them. For a time. Until one day..." She stopped, the memory hurting her so much.

She looked him in the face then, summoning the courage. "He had been on a mission to destroy a munitions factory. He didn't realize it, but it was built next to a children's home. There were hundreds of war refugee children and sick and hurt ones living there. Babies. None more than thirteen or fourteen. I could have been one of them."

She looked down at her feet, kicking at the wave grabbing for her toes, then back at him again. "That's when he realized war was not just hell. It was hell!"

Harry read her expression, his respect for Loche growing. "He took you and ran from it, didn't he?"

She nodded.

She looked back at him. "Now you will hate him for abandoning his duty."

Harry took her hands in his and pressed them tightly between his own. "I could never judge you or him. War is not a good bedfellow. Ever!"

She burst into tears.

He pulled her to him.

For the next few hours, the sun settled finally, but they didn't notice, they were lost in the wonder and exploration of each other. Her, remembering a body she had once known intimately and he, discovering that a woman was a woman in any world, or timeline, and that love didn't need to conform to any standards he had made. They needed each other then and that's all that mattered. Maybe all that ever would.

When they were finally through, they lay together close, lost in their own separate memories, but not of each other. He had his left arm around her shoulders, and she nuzzled her head into his shoulder. He could feel her sweet breath upon his cheek. It was gentle and sweet, like the lilacs he remembered of home.

That gave him a gut sinking feeling for a moment. Home. What was home? Would he ever reach it again? He had been thrust into a foreign future where Hitler dominated the world with battalions of super soldiers and exotic weapons that thrust any resistance aside. A world where zombies, robots and war machines dominated. Where love and hope were faint glimmers from the past.

Then he hardened. No. He wouldn't fall into that.

He sat up suddenly.

"Harry?" She asked urgently, concerned about his sudden movement.

She sat up too, took his hands in hers. He looked off at the horizon. In the distance storm clouds were gathering, bolts of lightning lit them. No sound of thunder reached them.

"It's not you. It's me. I hate what my life has become. What my world has become!"

She gave him a hurt look. "You hate being here with me?"

He regretted his vehemence immediately. "No. No. It's not you. It's me. I left a world ruled by a ruthless dictator who lobotomized his citizens then turned them into robots and zombies to feed his war machine. I refuse to believe I can't help fight that war any longer."

He stood up.

Flashes of light illuminated the beach from lightning bolts in the distance, but still no thunder.

He took her hands. "I've got to try and return home."

She stared into his eyes. "I've known from the first you could never stay, Harry. And I won't try to make you do so."

She broke free from his hands. She smiled. "It's your happiness I want. Not mine."

He was about to reply when a lightning bolt lit up the beach as bright as the sun. He spun about and the clouds were closer, and the sands on the beach were beginning to stir. He looked at the nearby grass and it was stiffening and trying to break free from its roots.

"Run!" He ordered her. "Tell Loche! Now!"

She gave him a frightened look. "No. I can't lose you again!"

He looked her in the eyes. "You will never lose me!" He promised.

He ran for the cave.

She started to follow.

"Loche!" He hollered over his shoulder. "Run!" He ordered again.

She ran into the forest as the mysterious clouds of lightning neared the beach, and bolts of energy began lancing downwards, striking the water, and turning it into vicious pools of turmoil and angry waterspouts.

Sky Captain

Loche looked up from the meal he had been preparing as a flash of bright light seared across the humble home he had built, letting in searing blazes of pure white. His eyes narrowed with anger and a touch of despair.

"Father!" Ilyana called out, and then burst into the home.

He swept her into his arms. She was sobbing. "Harry is going to...going to..."

He held her close. "It would seem our new Harry is not so different from the old one then, after all." He told her gently.

She looked up into his eyes and wiped at her own. "I don't want him to die."

"Men die. Women die. Such is life." He told her, plainly and simply. "It is the way of our world. All worlds."

A new burst of light seared the home, and then it became illuminated by an intense beam of light.

Loche and Ilyana ran outside.

Hovering over the home, high in the magnetic cloud disturbance overhead was another one of the strange flying boats.

"They have found us." He said simply.

Bolts of pure red energy struck the earth in front of their home, sending small explosions flaming debris towards them.

Loche threw Ilyana to the ground and covered her with his body as a second barrage struck, sending their home into the sky in a thousand pieces of flaming debris. He winced as pieces of burning wood and leaf struck his body and then began rolling over and over with Ilyana until they were clear of the worst of it.

They struggled to their feet as the vessel high overhead began to lower itself on blue beams of light.

"It's landing." He told Ilyana. "You must run. Run as you've never run before."

"No."

He turned to her. "You must!"

She stared blankly at him.

He nodded towards the woods nearby. "I am not so helpless as to let them take me without a..."

Before she could say more or he, they both heard this high-pitched whining sound. They looked up. Harry was in the old flying suit, arrowing towards the vessel in the sky.

Ilyana broke free of her father. "NO!" She cried out.

Promises Made

But Harry didn't hear her.

He was too busy trying to stay alive and to keep his promise. This time. At least this once.

As he closed in on the alien ship hovering over the destroyed home of Loche and Ilyana he saw the two of them racing into the woods. He smiled to himself. *At least they don't have to die or watch me die.* He said to himself with a grimace.

He chose that moment to loosen the Sky Captain suit arm he had retrieved for just such a time as now and activated its power sensors. It stiffened in his grip. Multiple missiles poked into view at its front.

"Now!" He said with a grin. "Let's see who dies today!"

He fired the missiles in a spread that launched them all at once. Six tiny, sub-nuclear warheads, devised by the smartest brains of his last world...Einstein and Tesla...fell through the air towards the alien ship.

"Kiss your asses goodbye!" Harry screamed and then veered off.

A second later his missiles struck.

The alien ship became a living vortex of nuclear energies that expanded outwards, reaching for Harry. He shot through the outer rim of the ascending energies and felt his body pulse as if it had become super energized for a moment, and then he burst free and launched towards the beach, away from the exploding vessel.

He risked looking back and saw the huge alien vehicle melting in the hellfire of his missiles, torn apart by numerous smaller explosions as even its most powerful body of metal and energy began to melt and fall to pieces.

Harry's power cut out.

He fell like a rock. Hard. Fast. Rock!

Darkness!

Darkness

"Harry wake up, Damnit!"

Harry struggled to wake up, but he didn't want to. He wanted to weep. He had won the battle but lost the war once more. Visions of Loche and Ilyana filled his heart and mind. Tears began to course down his face as he felt strong hands lift him gently and place him on something semi-hard.

He didn't open his eyes. He couldn't. Too much pain. Too much loss.

Darkness.

Lost and Found

Barry entered the infirmary, where Harry had been taken. They had found him wandering the slopes of the Swiss mountain fortress their base was built inside of. At first, they had thought it was a Nazi storm trooper, but when they saw the ancient Sky Captain suit, they had known otherwise immediately.

Harry was walking like a man lost forever. He wept incessantly. He held his helmet in the crook of one of his arms and kept looking around, as if seeking someone, or something.

Barry had been the first to reach him.

"Harry, wake up, Damnit!"

Harry had lost consciousness.

Barry had grunted like hell. It killed his back and arms, but he refused to let anyone lift Harry up and carry him. He struggled up the mountainside, his insides aching like hell. "Hang in there, Harry! Hang in there!"

He screamed at the soldiers on his left and right. "Damnit, why aren't you getting a doctor for him?"

Several of them ran up the slope.

Barry reached the secret entrance, the same time as Al and Nick came running out, followed by the only woman Harry had loved twice...once as his companion in World War Two and again after World War Three when he had been thrust from his own timeline and launched into an alternate timeline where Hitler had won World War Two and launched World War Three, bringing all of humanity to its knees.

Al and Nick insisted on placing Harry on the stretcher brought forth, relieving Barry of the weight. He had collapsed momentarily, but then struggled back to his feet. Harriet was weeping uncontrollably, her face telling it all. She feared Harry was going to die. It was dark and his body glowed. Glowed in the dark.

"You're one tough nut, Harry." Barry told his friend as he slid onto a chair next to his bed.

Harry just laid there; his eyes focused on a distant horizon only he could see.

Barry sighed. "Hairy, you gotta talk man. This is not helping anybody. Especially Harriet."

Harry's eyes refocused and he saw Barry next to him. He put a hand on Barry's knee. "I always have been and will be your friend, Barry."

Barry laughed. "Man, now you're beginning to sound like one of those dumb science fiction movie heroes."

Harry smiled and took his hand back.

Promises Kept

Barry came back to the infirmary later that night with Harriet. He found her sobbing. She looked at him. "He's gone, Barry."

Barry gave her a blank look. "Gone? How? Where?"

She shook her head, and he gathered her into his arms.

"Where?" He asked.

"Somewhere we can't go." She finally answered.

Home

On a distant island in the Pacific Harry zoomed across the skies, hurtling from a brief warp in time and space he had created with his new Sky Captain suit. It had adjustments that Al and Nick had made for him. He had made them promise not to tell anyone. He had told them his promise.

"You must do what's right, Harry." Al told him, his eyes warm with pride.

Nick nodded. "I remember when I loved like that once."

Then he grinned at Al. "Then I went and married her. Now everything's gone to hell!"

They both had laughed.

Harry cocked his helmet and saw infrared signatures of two humans below. He lowered the thrust of his suit and prepared to land.

He smiled. "Home."

Sky Captain's Son

Loche yawned, stretched, and lay down on his bed.

Ilyana smiled at him, and then went outside to sit on the porch they had constructed. It had kept them both busy, after rebuilding their home. They refused to let the forest reclaim it from them. They managed to salvage many parts of the older home and use them in the reconstruction, until finally it was finished.

They had looked at it and it somehow seemed hollow and empty.

That was when they decided to build the porch. Put off moving in. Put off the memories of their loss.

"Goodnight, Papa." She told Loche.

He had smiled. "And it is. A good night."

He had turned over to look the other way as someone entered the home.

Ilyana gasped. Fearful they had been invaded again.

But when she turned around her heart almost burst with joy. She felt her blood rushing to her face, her heart, and her hands. "Harry?"

He stood in the doorway grinning, contorting his face in his usual silly grin. "Man, why does it smell like crap in here?"

Loche grunted. "You'd know if you ever bothered to drop in more frequently."

Ilyana rushed into Harry's arms. He clasped her tight. Both wept for joy as they crushed against each other. The moment seemed to stretch forever until a tiny voice began to wail.

Harry pulled away.

Ilyana gave him a coy smile. "I think it's time you met someone, Harry."

She rushed to a corner beside Loche and lifted a small baby from a crib. She turned around and held it for Harry to see. "Our son!"

Time Clone

Harry stood outside amidst the palm trees and watched silently as he, or rather another time version of him, walked onto the porch and sat down. That Harry held a tiny baby. Harry held it up high and shook it lightly. The baby screamed with laughter.

Ilyana came out and sat next to Harry and nuzzled against him. He set the baby between them and leaned into them.

Loche came out and stood behind them. But he wasn't looking at them; he was looking into the palm trees. When he finally spotted what he had been looking for, he gave a big smile.

Harry waved from his hiding place, and then slipped back into the jungle. He hurried back to where he had set aside his Sky Captain suit and then hurriedly climbed into it. He kept the power at the lowest setting, so he didn't disturb the reunion going on with the other Harry and the ones he loved so much.

As he launched away from the island, he remembered his last conversation with Al. It had been very late at night. Harriet had sat next to him, anxious and worried. He wanted to do what was right for her, as well as the ones he had left behind. He also wanted her to know what he had done. What part of him remained behind?

She had cried a long time and rushed off, angry as hell at him, but unknown to him she had returned to lean on the entrance to Al's office and listened as Harry told the story of everything that had happened and what he wanted to do.

Al had seen her but said nothing. He wanted Harry to finish.

Finished, Harry stood, anguish on his face. "I love Harriet more than life itself. But I also love Ilyana. What else can I do? I can't be the same man to both?"

Al had nodded, motioning Harriet to stay when she seemed ready to come in. "I think you know that if you break the rules of time and space there could be a penalty."

"You mean I could die twice?" Harry quipped; his face deadly serious. "I've already died more than once already. It doesn't get any easier."

Al shook his head, took a puff off his pipe, and then shook it at Harry. "Son, I'm not God and I don't pretend to be, but I would imagine if I were, I wouldn't like to leave untidy messes behind me."

"Are you calling Ilyana an untidy mess?"

Al put a hand on Harry's shoulder and gave him a warm smile. "No, Harry, I'm calling you an untidy mess. You are an honorable man caught in the cross hairs of things beyond the imagination of most men and women. It takes a strong man to deal with that. You are that man. Never forget it. Once you remember who you really are, you will never be an untidy mess. To you or anyone else."

That was when Harriet stepped into the office.

Harry turned around, surprised. "I'm sorry..."

She shut his mouth with a finger. "Shut your mouth. Don't ever apologize for being the good man you are. Never."

He pulled the finger away. "I..."

She shut his mouth with a kiss.

Al smiled and took the cue to exit his office. He shut the door behind him.

Harry approached the zone of entropy he had encountered last time he had plunged to earth and gone cross time streams. He hadn't realized it the first time, his attention had been on the bomber, but now he was.

He pressed his accelerator to the max and shot into the zone. Vanished.

On the porch of the hut, Loche looked up and the others at the sound of something breaking the sound barrier and then the time barrier.

Unseen by Ilyana, Harry mouthed these words. "God bless you, Harry."

"Hey!" He laughed as the baby began to squeal with laughter again.

Harry had crossed the time streams and caught him before he could die smashing into the ship. Yes, he had really died, but Harry had taken him from the time stream before his final death. It was what had worried the duplicate Harry so much. What would it do to both their realities? What would be the penalty?

When Harry had landed with himself at the cave, he had immediately seen that his suit was missing. "You used it."

Harry had nodded to his self. "Had to."

"I understand, Harry." He had told himself.

They both smiled at each other.

"This is going to be really awkward if Ilyana finds us together at the same time." Harry had told himself.

"I know." The other Harry had agreed at once.

So, they had separated. He had headed back to the hut and the other Harry had set off to watch them together before leaving.

Harry looked into Ilyana's eyes. "Let's play a game."

"Okay. What is it?" She asked, as their baby looked at both.

"Guess my secret."

Ilyana laughed.

Allied Base

Harry shot from the zone of entropy and emerged about a hundred miles south of the Allied Defense base in Switzerland. He turned on his earpiece.

"Barry, you copy me?"

Static.

"Barry?"

Static.

He began to grow extremely worried.

"Barry, do you copy me? Over."

Static, then. "Hey big guy, do I ever got a surprise for you?" Harriet's voice came through into his helmet.

He grinned.

"What is it?"

"Let's play a game."

"Okay, what is it?"

"Guess my secret."

Harry burst into laughter so deep and rich that he almost broke into tears. He poured on the juice and headed for home. Home.9

Home!

Get a Free Book from me.

Learn more about my Sherlock Holmes in the back of this book in the glossary. It will help you to understand the new world I have placed Sherlock Holmes within and those he deals with.

I describe most of my characters and the world the new Sherlock Holmes solves his cases.

Grab a free Sherlock Holmes book on me![1]

Author's Note

If you want to keep abreast of the latest news, follow me on my author site: www.bakerstreetuniverses.com

Connect with me on Twitter: @johnpirillo

Friend me at my Facebook page: John Pirillo, Author[2].

Join my Baker Street Universe group to get things I don't usually share with others, and to hash over the universe I've created with me and fellow authors and readers. I'll be having incredibly special giveaways, advance copies, and autographed work as well as other surprises to my friends who join me there.

My artwork is available at: https://john-pirillo.pixels.com/

---

2.   https://www.facebook.com/john.pirillo.3.

OTHER BOOKS BY THE AUTHOR

SHERLOCK HOLMES, MAMMOTH FANTASY, MURDER AND MYSTERY TALES 21

SHERLOCK HOLMES, MAMMOTH FANTASY, MURDER AND MYSTERY TALES 22

SHERLOCK HOLMES, MAMMOTH FANTASY, MURDER AND MYSTERY TALES 23

SHERLOCK HOLMES, MAMMOTH FANTASY, MURDER AND MYSTERY TALES 24

SHERLOCK HOLMES, MAMMOTH FANTASY, MURDER AND MYSTERY TALES 25

SHERLOCK HOLMES, MAMMOTH FANTASY, MURDER AND MYSTERY TALES 26

SHERLOCK HOLMES, MAMMOTH FANTASY, MURDER, AND MYSTERY TALES 27

SHERLOCK HOLMES, MAMMOTH FANTASY, MURDER, AND MYSTERY TALES 28

SHERLOCK HOLMES, MOST PECULIAR

SHIFTERS+

SHIFTERS2+

DOUBLE HOLMES 2

ABNOMALIES

BAKER STREET WIZARD

BAKER STREET WIZARD 2

BAKER STREET WIZARD 3

DEEP SILENCE

DOUBLE HOLMES

DOUBLE HOLMES 2

DOUBLE HOLMES 3

DOUBLE HOLMES 4
DOUBLE HOLMES 5
DOUBLE HOLMES 6
DOUBLE HOLMES 7
DOUBLE HOLMES 8
DOUBLE HOLMES 9
DOUBLE HOLMES 10
DOUBLE HOLMES 11
DOUBLE HOLMES 12
DOUBLE HOLMES 13
DOUBLE HOLMES 14
DOUBLE HOLMES 15
FORBIDDEN WORLD
GEARS WORLD
GEARS WORLD 2
GEARS WORLD 3
GEARS WORLD 4
GEARS WORLD 5
GEARS WORLD 6
HALLOWEEN TREATS
JOURNEY INTO THE UNKNOWN
JOURNEY TO THE CENTER OF THE EARTH
JOURNEY
JOURNEY 2
JOURNEY 3
MONSTER HUNTER
ROCKET MAN TIME STREAMS 2
ROCKET MAN, PHOENIX
ROCKET MAN, THE SECRET WAR
ROCKET MAN, TIME STREAMS
ROCKETMAN, ARCH OF TIME
SECRET ADVENTURES OF JULES VERNE AND

ALEXANDER DUMAS, THE SEA DEMON
SECRET ADVENTURES OF JULES VERNE AND
ALEXANDER DUMAS, HOLLOW EARTH
SHERLOCK HOLMES, BAKER STREET WIZARD
SHERLOCK HOLMES, BAKER STREET WIZARD 2
SHERLOCK HOLMES, BAKER STREET WIZARD 3
SHERLOCK HOLMES, BAKER STREET WIZARD 4
SHERLOCK HOLMES, BAKER STREET WIZARD 5
SHERLOCK HOLMES, BAKER STREET WIZARD 5
SHERLOCK HOLMES, BLACK WIZARD
SHERLOCK HOLMES, CURSE OF THE BLACK WIZARD
SHERLOCK HOLMES, DEADLY MASTER
SHERLOCK HOLMES, HALLOWEEN VAMPIRE TALES
SHSERLOCK HOLMES, WEREWOLVE TALES
SHERLOCK HOLMES, HALLOWEEN MONSTERS
SHERLOCK HOLMES, HALLOWEEN MONSTERS 2
SHERLOCK HOLMES, LORD OF THE TREES
SHERLOCK HOLMES, THE BAKER STREET UNIVERSE
SHERLOCK HOLMES, URBAN FANTASY MYSTERIES
SHERLOCK HOLMES, URBAN FANTASY MYSTERIES 2
SHERLOCK HOLMES, URBAN FANTASY MYSTERIES 3
SHIFTER 1-4
THE CTHULHU INCIDENT 1-5
SKY CAPTAIN 1-3

Don't miss out!

Visit the website below and you can sign up to receive emails whenever John Pirillo publishes a new book. There's no charge and no obligation.

https://books2read.com/r/B-A-EMSD-EGJQC

BOOKS 2 READ

Connecting independent readers to independent writers.

Did you love *Sky Captain Adventures 3*? Then you should read *Sky Captain Adventures 2, Zombie World* by John Pirillo!

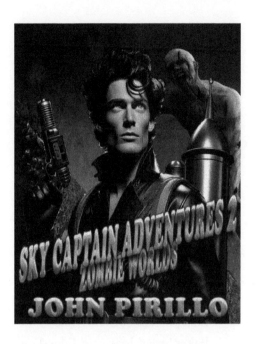

Sky Captain can fly faster than sound......faster than light.

Now he is flying into three more exciting, action-packed adventures.

SUPER SOLDIER

Hitler has hired the diabolical Doctor Zombie to build totally obedient and powerful soldiers made of flesh and metal.

DOCTOR ZOMBIE

Not content with his progress, Doctor Zombie is now hard wiring human beings to obey his orders.

THE ZOMBIE FACTORY

Sky Captain and his best friend Barry have been captured by Doctor Zombie...and his plans for them are worse than death!

Three action packed adventures of a new kind of superhero caught in a time loop that has separated him from the woman he loves and

everything he cared for.

Can he ever get home again?

Read more at www.johnpirillo.com.

Also by John Pirillo

Angel Hamilton
Broken Fangs

Baker Street Universe Tales
Baker Street Universe Tales
Baker Street Universe Tales 2
Baker Street Universe Tales 3
Baker Street Universe Tales 4
Baker Street Universe Tales 5
Baker Street Universe Tales 6
Baker Street Universe Tales Seven

BAKER STREET WIZARD
Baker Street Wizard 4
Baker Street Wizard 5

Between
Prince of Between

"Classic Baker Street Universe Sherlock Holmes"
Sherlock Holme: Hyde's Night of Terror
Case of the Deadly Goddess
Case of the Abominable

Cythulhu
The Cthulhu Incident
The Eye of Cthulhu
The Throne of Cythulhu
Throne of Cthulhu
Giants of Cythulhu

Deadly
Sherlock Holmes, Deadly Master
Sherlock Holmes, Deadly Magic

Detective Judge Dee
Detective Dee Murder Most Chaste

Double Holmes
Sherlock Holmes, Double Holmes 2
Double Holmes 7
Double Holmes 8
Double Holmes 9
Double Holmes 10
Double Holmes 11
Double Holmes 12

Double Holmes 13
Double Holmes 14
Double Holmes 15
Double Holmes 16

Elektron
Elektron

Escape To Adventure
Escape to Adventure
Escape to Atlantis

FRACTAL UNIVERSE
Twist
Portal

G1, The Bureau of Extraordinary Investigations
Shifter 2+
Shifter 3+

Gears World
Gears World 5

Halloween
Sherlock Holmes, Halloween Monsters 2

Halloween Treats
Sherlock Holmes, Halloween Vampire Tales
Sherlock Holmes, Halloween Werewolf Tales

Hollow Earth Special Forces
Hollow Earth Special Forces, Forbidden World
Operation Deep Thrust
The Ancients

Holmes
Sherlock Holmes Struck
Sherlock Holmes A Dangerous Act

Infinite Tales
Infinite Tales 3
Infinite Tales 4
Infinite Tales 5
Infinite Tales 6
Infinite Tales 7
Infinite 8
Infinite Tales 9
Infinite Tales
Infinite Tales Two

Monster Hunter
Monster Hunter

Mystery Knight
HellBound Mystery
Hell Bound Angel

PhaseShift
PhaseShift
PhaseShift Two: Crossover
PhaseShift: Shifting Worlds

Rocketman
Rocketman
Rocket Man, Time Streams
Rocketman Christmas
Time Wars
Arch of Time

Secret Adventures of Jules Verne and Alexander Dumas
Hollow Earth
Hollow Earth

Sherlock Holmes
Sherlock Holmes, ICE
The Ice Man
Sherlock Holmes Fallen
Sherlock Holmes: Monster
Sherlock Holmes: Tick Tock
Sherlock Holmes Christmas Magic

Sherlock Holmes Dark Secret
Sherlock Holmes Shadow of Dorian Gray
Sherlock Holmes Vampire
Sherlock Holmes: Cursed in Stone
Sherlock Holmes Apparition
Sherlock Holmes Case of the Raging Madness
Sherlock Holmes Dark Princess
Sherlock Holmes Dark Angel
Constable Evans' Fancy
Sherlock Holmes Matter of Perception
Sherlock Holmes Tangled
Sherlock Holmes Case of the Gossamer Lady
Sherlock Holmes House of Shadows
Sherlock Holmes The Yellow Death
Sherlock Holmes Oblique
Sherlock Holmes Mystery Train Winter Collection
Sherlock Holmes A Tale Less Told
Sherlock Holmes Mystery Six
Sherlock Holmes, Rules of Darkness, Special Edition
Sherlock Holmes Shape of Justice
Sherlock Holmes Christmas Magic
Sherlock Holmes Fallen Angel
Ghostly Shadows
Sherlock Holmes Bloody Hell
Sherlock Holmes Monster of the Tower
Sherlock Holmes Darkest of Nights
Sherlock Holmes Nightmare
Sherlock Holmes Poetry of Death
Sherlock Holmes, Dracula
Sherlock Holmes #3, Ice Storm
Sherlock Holmes, Baker Street Wizard 3

Sherlock Holmes Double Holmes
Sherlock Holmes, Double Holmes 1

Sherlock Holmes, Mammoth Fantasy, Murder and Mystery Tales
Sherlock Holmes, Mammoth Fantasy, Murder, and Mystery Tales 15
Sherlock Holmes Mammoth Fantasy, Murder, and Mystery Tales 17
Sherlock Holmes Mammoth Fantasy, Murder, and Mystery Tales 26
Sherlock Holmes Mammoth Fantasy, Murder, and Mystery Tales 14

Sherlock Holmes, Mammoth Fantasy, Murder, and Mystery Tales 15
Sherlock, Holmes, Mammoth Fantasy, Murder, and Mystery Tales 15

Sherlock Holmes Urban Fantasy Mysteries
Sherlock Holmes Urban Fantasy Mysteries
Sherlock Holmes, Halloween Monsters
Sherlock Holmes Urban Fantasy Mysteries 2
Sherlock Holmes Urban Fantasy Mysteries 3
Sherlock Holmes, Urban Fantasy Mysteries 3
Sherlock Holmes Urban Fantasy Mysteries 4
Sherlock Holmes, Artifact
Sherlock Holmes, The Dracula Files
Sherlock Holmes, Dark Clues
Sherlock Holmes, Case of the Undying Man
Sherlock Holmes, Mystery of the Sea
Sherlock Holmes, Night Watch
Sherlock Holmes, Mystery of the Path not Taken
Sherlock Holmes, the Dorian Gray Affair
The Baker Street Universe
Sherlock Holmes, The Dracula Affair
Spector
Sherlock Holmes, Rules of Darkness
Sherlock Holmes, A Tale Less Told
Sherlock Holmes, The Christmas Star

Sherlock Holmes, Christmas Tales
Steampunk Holmes
Sherlock HOlmes, Deadly Valentine's Day
Sherlock Holmes, Angel Murders
Sherlock Holmes, Deadly Intent
Sherlock Holmes, White Diamond Mystery
Sherlock Holmes, Gears World, Box Set One
Sherlock Holmes, The Blue Fire of Harry Houdini
Sherlock Holmes, White Diamond Vampire Mystery
Sherlock Holmes, Black Tower
Sherlock Holmes, Tales of the Macabre
Sherlock Holmes, Baker Street Wizard
Sherlock Holmes, Usher
Sherlock Holmes, Baker Street Wizard 2
Sherlock Holmes, Double Holmes 1
Sherlock Holmes, Cave of the Dark Elf
Sherlock Holmes, Something Wicked
Sherlock Holmes, Gears Word 3
Sherlock Holmes, Gears World 4
Sherlock Holmes, Deadly
Sherlock Holmes, Urban Fantasy Mysteries Six
Werewolves
Sherlock Holmes, Mammoth Fantasy, Murder, and Mystery Tales 27
Sherlock Holmes, Urban Fantasy Mysteries
Sherlock Holmes, Lord of the Trees
Sherlock Holmes, The Ghost Wars, Book One, Rise of the Ghost Empire

Sherlock Holmes, Urban Fantasy Mystery Tales
Sherlock Holmes, Urban Fantasy Mystery Tales 2
Sherlock Holmes, Dark Matters
Sherlock Holmes, Black Wizard
Sherlock Holmes, Curse of the Black Wizard
Sherlock Holmes, The Ghost Wars, Book Two: The War of Magic

Sky Captain Adventures
Sky Captain Adventures 2, Zombie World
Sky Captain Adventures 3

Steampunk Holmes
Sherlock Holmes, Gears of the Goddess

The Baker Street Detective
The Baker Street Detective 5, The Howling Wind
Strange Times, The Baker Street Detective, Book2
The Baker Street Detective, Hollow Man
Sherlock Holmes, Baker Street Detectives

Thrilling Mystery Tales
Thrilling Mystery Tales 2

Twist
Twist 2
Twister

Urban Fantasies
Urban Fantasies 1
Urban Fantasies 3
Urban Fantasies

War of the Worlds
Battle for Earth

WireShip
Wirestation Red Lion

Standalone
Sherlock Holmes Deadly Consequences
Invisibility Factor
Red Painted Souls
Between
Robin Hood
Shadow Man
The Rainbow Bridge
Cartoon, Johnnie Angel
Sherlock Holmes 221B
Sherlock Holmes Shape Shifter
Urban Fantasy Mysteries
Sherlock Holmes, Urban Fantasy Mysteries
Halloween Mysteries
Invasion
Romancing the Word
Romancing the Word Workbook
Sherlock Holmes, Gears World 2
Thrilling Mystery Tales
Weird Short Tales
Spectre Forces
Young King Arthur
Dark Midnight
Anomalies

Shifter+
Shifter 4+
Deep Silence
Sherlock Holmes, Halloween Fantasies
Sherlock Holmes, Halloween Terror
Sherlock Holmes, Halloween Terror 2

Watch for more at www.johnpirillo.com.

Milton Keynes UK
Ingram Content Group UK Ltd.
UKHW011100201123
432908UK00007B/1439